Rocket

MOTLEY'S CREW

Smudger and the Smelly Fish

Margaret Ryan &
Margaret Chamberlain

A & C Black • London

Rockets series:

CROOK CATCHERS - Karen Wallace & Judy Brown

MOTLEY'S CREW - Margaret Ryan &
Margaret Chamberlain

MR CROC - Frank Rodgers

MRS MAGIC - Wendy Smith

MY FUNNY FAMILY - Colin West

ROVER - Chris Powling & Scoular Anderson

SILLY SAUSAGE - Michaela Morgan & Dee Shulman

WIZARD'S BOY - Scoular Anderson

First paperback edition 2001
First published 2001 in hardback by
A & C Black (Publishers) Ltd
35 Bedford Row, London WC1R 4JH

Text copyright © 2001 Margaret Ryan
Illustrations copyright © 2001 Margaret Chamberlain

The right of Margaret Ryan and Margaret Chamberlain
to be identified as author and illustrator of this
work has been asserted by them in accordance
with the Copyright, Designs and Patents Act 1988.

ISBN 0-7136-5460-0

A CIP catalogue record for this book is available
from the British Library.

Printed and bound by G. Z. Printek, Bilbao, Spain.

Chapter One

Smudger, the first mate of the pirate ship, *Hesmeralda*, was up in the crow's nest, painting. He painted his clothes. He painted his nose. He would have painted the crows if they hadn't flapped away sharpish.

'Cor Blimey!' they cawed.

But Smudger didn't care. He liked being messy.

4

'MESSY FOR YOU. I MEAN MESSAGE FOR YOU,' squawked Squawk, the ship's parrot.

'What!' yelled Smudger, and dropped his paint pot straight onto the head of Kevin, the cabin boy, who was sunning himself on the deck below.

And Smudger slid down the mast double-quick and landed in the large pot of porridge Doris, the cook, had left out to cool.

My mum's coming on a visit. I've got to get clean!

Don't worry Smudger, we'll help you.

The Captain, Kevin and Doris filled up the ship's bathtub and plonked Smudger in.

'What a lot of fuss you make, Smudger,' said the Captain, and scrubbed his back with a deck brush.

'What a lot of fuss you make, Smudger,' said Doris, and gave him a porridge facepack.

'What a lot of fuss you make, Smudger,'
said Kevin, and soaped his hair with his
very own Pirate Pete shampoo.

Smudger jumped out of the tub and ran
around on deck.

13

Smudger scurried below decks and came back five minutes later wearing a clean shirt and trousers. He even had a clean hanky in his pocket.

Smudger scowled and threw a towel at Squawk.

'Shut up, smart beak,' he muttered. 'You know quite well it's me.'

Chapter Two

Smudger got clean just in time as LEFT RIGHT LEFT RIGHT LEFT RIGHT... up the gangplank marched his mum.

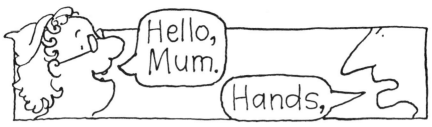

'Hands,' said his mum. Smudger held
them out to be inspected.

'Neck,' said his mum. Smudger held it
out to be inspected.

'Ears,' said his mum and nearly yanked
them off. But they were clean.

Er hi, Mrs er Smudge er mum. How are you?

I'm fine, but you've got a hole in your sock. Darn it immediately. Then get this ship cleaned. All of you. I want it sparkling.

Smudger cleaned the deck. Kevin cleaned the portholes. Captain Motley polished the ship's wheel. Smudger's mum stood over them while they worked, and tapped her foot.

Squawk hid up in the crow's nest.

JUST LISTEN TO THE TAPPING OF HER FEET, BUT THE HESMERALDA'S NEVER BEEN SO NEAT.

THOUGH SMUDGER'S MUM REALLY IS A TARTAR,

THE CREW AND THE SHIP HAVE NEVER LOOKED SMARTER!

But someone else was keeping an eye on all the cleaning up. Captain Motley's arch-enemy, Captain Horatio Thunderguts, was standing on the deck of his ship, the *Saucy Stew*, peering through his spyglass.

'What's going on aboard the *Hesmeralda*?' he muttered.
'First Smudger has a bath and it's not the first Tuesday in the New Year, then the ship gets cleaned from bow to stern.

They're up to something, I'll be bound. But whatever it is, I'll soon put a stop to it, or my name's not Horatio Thunderguts.'

Meantime, on board a sparkling *Hesmeralda*, Captain Motley was offering Smudger's mum afternoon tea.

'Only the best for you, silly old bat,'
muttered Doris.

'I wouldn't do that,' said Kevin.

The Captain got out the best china with A PRESENT FROM DEADMAN'S COVE written on it. Doris made tea and proper scones while Kevin put out the napkins. Smudger didn't know what to do so he blew his nose on his clean hanky just to let his mum see he had one.

Well done, Smudger.

'Well done indeed,' said the Chief Pirate coming up the gangplank. 'I saw all the cleaning going on and I thought I would come on board to congratulate you. What a smart crew on a smart ship. You're a credit to the fleet.'

And he sat down beside Smudger's mum.
Squawk rolled his eyes.

Chapter Three

Back on board the *Saucy Stew*,
Captain Horatio Thunderguts was
not happy. It was easy to tell. He
jumped up and down on the deck.
He jumped up and down on his hat.
He would have jumped up and
down on the ship's cat if it hadn't
shot away sharpish. Then he yelled,
'I AM NOT HAPPY!'

AND DO YOU KNOW WHY?

Got belly ache?

(The captain ate rather a lot of fish heads.)

NO!

Got jelly ache?

(The captain ate rather a lot of jellied eels.)

NO!

Got smelly ache?

(The captain's feet ponged a bit.)

NO!

What then? Give us a clue.

There's something going on aboard the Hesmeralda. First Smudger has a bath, then the ship gets cleaned, now they're all having afternoon tea with Smudger's mum and the Chief Pirate and **THEY DIDN'T INVITE ME!**

We could invite the Chief Pirate to have afternoon tea with us.

The captain peered again through his spyglass.

Chapter Four

Afternoon tea on the *Hesmeralda* was going very well. The Captain talked about the weather. Doris talked about her new porridge recipes, and Smudger's mum talked about what a lovely baby Smudger had been. She was just handing round her photos of the tiny Smudger when the much larger Smudger heard a noise.

Did you hear that noise?

'I'm sure I heard a noise,' said Smudger. 'It must be because my ears are so clean.' And he went to investigate. He tiptoed round the wheel house and was just in time to see Captain Horatio Thunderguts empty a bucketful of smelly fish heads onto the *Hesmeralda*'s clean deck. And he was laughing...

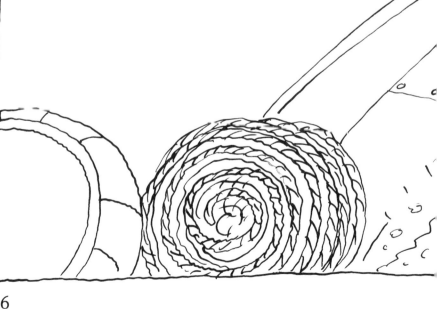

Smudger rushed towards Captain Thunderguts... but... CRASH BANG WALLOP... he slid on the smelly fish heads, skidded across the deck and banged his head on the ship's side.

'Getting away?' cried Smudger's mum. 'We'll soon see about that.' And she grabbed a coil of rope and lassoed Thunderguts as he clambered over the side.

OOH, AAH, HELP! LEMME GO! LEMME GO!

'As you wish,' said Smudger's mum and dropped him in the sea.

'Make up your mind,' grinned Smudger's mum, and hauled him back on board.

'Really amazing. We must talk about that... over dinner perhaps, but first let's see who you've lassoed...'

'Oh no, please don't, Chief Pirate,' begged Thunderguts. 'Then I'd have to get a proper job. Please don't throw me out of the fleet.'

'Very well,' said the Chief Pirate. 'Then I shall ask Smudger's mum if she'll go aboard the *Saucy Stew* and smarten you all up.'

Captain Horatio Thunderguts' face turned white, and he shook like a wobbly jelly.

'You'll do as you're told,' said Smudger's mum. 'Now get back to the *Saucy Stew* immediately. I want that deck so clean I could eat my dinner off it. I want those portholes so clean I can see my face in them, and I want the crew so clean they squeak when they walk. Now MOVE!'

And she marched Thunderguts LEFT RIGHT LEFT RIGHT LEFT RIGHT all the way back to the *Saucy Stew*.

Smudger, who was sitting up in among the smelly fish heads, grinned and started to pick them up. When he had finished, his face was dirty, his clothes were dirty and he smelled awful.

The Captain and crew of the *Hesmeralda* didn't mind. They grinned and held their noses.

Now that's more like our first mate.

Smudger wiped his fishy hands on the seat of his trousers.

'I like being messy,' he said.